Denise Freiher Burnette

The Day The Sun Went Out in Grown-Upsville

Written by Denise Fuehrer Burnette
Illustrated by Ann Adams

A "Create" Publication
Caswell County, NC

Denise Fuehrer Burnette is a writer, poet, dancer, and dabbler in many things creative. She received an MA from the California Institute of Integral Studies where she studied East/West Psychology with a concentration in Creativity. She is the author of "The Fire Beneath your Feet," a collection of poetry inspiring others to trust their own creative fire and share it with the world. Passionate about the healing and transformative power of creativity, she is currently the Executive Director of the Caswell Council for the Arts. She enjoys writing, dancing, poetry, playing disc golf, hiking, and spending time with her family and friends. She lives in Caswell County, North Carolina with her husband Rich and their two children, Treya and Richard.

Ann Adams is a visual and performing artist who lives in Raleigh, NC. She studied visual arts at Meredith College and went on to become an art educator in the wake county public schools for 30 years. After retiring in 2015, she is currently a free-lance artist specializing in painting and design graphics for clothing. A master tie dye artist, she uses her dyed fabrics as backgrounds for much of her work. After performing in a rock band "the blenders" for 11 years, she has shifted focus to now developing and playing original music. She enjoys teaching and practicing yoga, writing and blogging about what it means to be human, biking, playing disc golf and spending quality time with her family. She has 2 grown children and a husband of 32 years. She considers herself a possibilitarian and is open to learning and studying new things but most importantly sharing new ideas.

This book is dedicated to the inner child in us all, and to the children in our lives who are a constant reminder to live in the moment and enjoy this life we are given.

And to our own children

Treya & Richard
Anna Grace & James Darden

You have taught us more than you could ever imagine.

Let me tell you a story about a little town on top of a big hill, a town called Grown-Upsville.

The people of Grown-Upsville worked very hard.

3

They woke up early every morning when the rooster crowed and they worked all day until the sun set.

Then they would
go back to their
homes on the
top of the hill to
rest.

They were very proud of their hard work. So proud, in fact, that they never, ever took a day off. They all had pretty homes and fancy cars and many of them had boats and airplanes too. How lucky we are, they thought, look at all of the wonderful things that we have because we work so hard.

Oh, I almost forgot to mention something very important about the people who lived in Grown-upsville. They were all grown-ups!

One morning, when the people of Grown-Upsville woke up in their comfy beds in their pretty homes at the top of the hill, they found that it was still dark out. Everyone was surprised. It seemed that the Sun should have been up by now.

They all looked at their shiny clocks, and their shiny clocks said it was time for the Sun to come out. They were confused.

They waited and waited, but still no Sun. Then, one by one, they took their fancy lanterns and met in the center of town. Together they waited all day long, but still no Sun.

They began to worry.

"Oh my, how will I ever grow my crops if the Sun does not come out?" said the farmer.

"How will I deliver the mail in the dark?" worried the mail carrier.

"What will we do if the Sun never comes out again?" they all wondered.

That night the town council had an emergency meeting and everyone in the town was there.

All of the greatest scientists, weather forecasters, astrologers, and astrono-mers, the smartest people of Grown-Upsville all met and tried to figure out why the Sun had not come out.

Some thought maybe the Sun had burned out. Others thought perhaps it had taken a wrong turn in the galaxy and would never be seen again.

There was an outsider at the town meeting that night, someone who did not live in Grown-Upsville. Johnny Kidd, the grandson of Harvey Elder, was there visiting his grandpa. Right in the middle of this most important meeting, Johnny Kidd stood up, much to his grandfather's surprise, and began to speak.

"Hello, my name is Johnny Kidd, and I've been visiting you folks here in Grown-Upsville for about a week now. I think that I know why the Sun has not come out today, and I think I know how we can get it to come back."

Now typically the people of Grown-Upsville might not bother listening to the advice of a kid. But since they were in great need of a solution, they let the boy speak.

"Every day in Grown-Upsville you get up at the crack of dawn to go to work. When the Sun goes down, you come home and rest so that you will be ready to work hard again the next day.   No one ever takes the time to go outside and play with the Sun. It is no wonder that the Sun does not want to come around here anymore. It doesn't feel loved and appreciated. If I was the Sun, I don't think I would come around here anymore either."

Johnny finished speaking and the room was silent. Maybe Johnny was right, they all thought, maybe the Sun had decided not to come back because they never showed that they loved it.

What a great friend the Sun had always been. It rose every morning like clockwork, giving them light and heat so they could live. They had always taken the Sun for granted, and now it was gone.

"So what should we do?" they asked.

"I have an idea." said Johnny. "Tomorrow, we must have a special day to honor the Sun. We must all rise up very early from bed and meet out on the hillside to wait for it to rise. We will promise the Sun that if it comes back to Grown-Upsville, we will not work all day long. Instead, we will spend the day outside playing with the Sun."

They took a vote and everyone agreed. Now all they could do was wait.

Very early the next morn-
ing, everyone in the town
was awake and ready.
They all sat together at the
top of the hill to see if the
Sun would return, and they
waited...

All of a sudden, the sky began to turn beautiful colors. Blue and purple and pink were everywhere.

"Here it comes!" yelled Johnny.

Everyone was amazed. Inch by inch, the Sun lifted itself over the horizon and high up into the sky, painting the country-side with colors and lights of every shade.

The people of Grown-Upsville were so happy to see the Sun again. They played and laughed with the Sun all day long.

And when the Sun set that evening, everyone in town sat together and said good-bye, thanking it for a wonderful day, and hoping it would come out again soon.

From that day on, the people of Grown-Upsville never forgot how special the Sun was to them. Once a week, even now, they have a special day to honor the Sun. Instead of working, they play outside and celebrate with the Sun all day long. And they call this special day Sunday so they will never forget how this very special day began.

THE END

39

CPSIA information can be obtained
at www.ICGtesting.com
Printed in the USA
LVHW071304141121
703219LV00004B/33